Chapter 1

Have you ever wished you could read people's minds? Tune into their heads and hear exactly what they're thinking? Well, forget it. You wouldn't like it. I know. I did it. And it wasn't a big treat at all. Believe me.

I guess I should begin at the beginning. My name is Zack. I'm ten years old. I live in New York City. And I'm in the fifth grade at the Horace Hyde-White School for Boys.

Ever since I was young, I've been interested in weird stuff. I don't think I'm weird myself. But I keep wishing that aliens would invite me onto their spaceship. Or that I could float out of my body and travel far away without stopping at gas station restrooms, which are always pretty gross.

Science is probably my favorite subject. It teaches you stuff that is at least as weird as reading minds. For example, do you know what a tachyon is? A tachyon is one of the tiniest things in the universe. Tinier than an atom, even. And it travels faster than the speed of light. A tachyon travels so fast, it gets where it's going before it starts out. If you were a tachyon, you'd never be late to school. You'd get there before you left home. I learned that in science class.

The time I want to tell you about happened in science class. Mrs. Coleman-Levin is my science teacher. She's also my homeroom teacher. She's kind of weird, but not in a bad way. For one thing, she always wears work boots. Even in summer. Even at dress-up parties at school in the evening. For another thing, she works weekends at the morgue. She does autopsies. That means cutting up dead people to see what they died of. Gross. But interesting.

Our classroom has a lot of weird, interesting stuff in it. There's a complete human skeleton hanging in the corner. Not a plastic model, either. It's a real one. On her desk, Mrs. Coleman-Levin keeps a glass jar with a pig brain in it. And we have lots of class pets. But not the cute, furry kind. We have a piranha fish and a tarantula and a snake. The piranha eats goldfish. The snake eats mice, which is kind of gross. Mrs. Coleman-Levin feeds them when we're not around. I don't think it bothers her at all.

On the day I want to tell you about, Mrs. Coleman-Levin was helping us do an experiment. It was with small electric motors. I was hooking one up. By accident, one of the wires fell into a beaker of water. Without thinking, I reached in and pulled it out. Suddenly my hand got all tingly. I felt as if sparks were shooting out of me.

"Zack!" Mrs. Coleman-Levin came rushing over to me. "Are you all right?"

"Uh, sure. Sort of," I said.

I really couldn't tell at that point, if you want to know the truth. I was too busy watching the little fireworks that were going off—Pop! Pop!—right in front of my eyes. Then I totally blacked out.

Chapter 2

"How are you feeling, dear?" said a strange, echoey voice.

It was the school nurse, Mrs. Krump. Her voice doesn't usually echo.

"Fine, thanks," I said. I always answer "Fine, thanks," even when I'm not. I've found that when people ask you how you are, they don't really want to know. They only want you to say you're fine so they can get on to the next thing.

"By the way," I said, "why am I here?"

"Don't you remember?" said Mrs. Krump in her echoey voice.

"Sure. Sort of," I said. "But tell me anyway."

"Well, you got an electric shock in science class," she said. "You put your hand in a beaker of water that had live wires in it. It knocked you out."

"Oh, right," I said. "I remember that."

And then a strange thing happened. Although her lips didn't move, I thought I heard Mrs. Krump say, *Stupid klutz. You're lucky you didn't electrocute yourself.*

"Excuse me?" I said.

"What?" said Mrs. Krump.

"You just called me a stupid klutz."

Mrs. Krump's face turned bright red.

"I said no such thing," she replied. And

then, although her lips weren't moving at all, I heard her say, *Must've been muttering under my breath. Better watch it.*

I don't know how she did it. Maybe she was a ventriloquist.

"How did you do that?" I asked.

"How did I do what?"

"Say what you just said without moving your lips."

Mrs. Krump frowned. She gave me a funny look. She made me lie down for fifteen minutes. She stuck a thermometer in my mouth. Then she said, "Zack, you do not have any fever. And you don't seem to be badly hurt. Would you like to go on to your next class?"

"OK," I said.

If I had remembered what my next class was, I probably wouldn't have said OK.

Chapter 3

My next class was geography. I like geography a lot. But we were having this big test that day. And I forgot to take my geography book home with me to study. So I was pretty much out of luck.

Our geography teacher, Mr. Snodgrass, passed out sheets with the test questions. I took a look at mine and started feeling dizzy. The first question was, "Name the two biggest rivers in Iraq."

My heart sank like a stone. I didn't have a clue. I wasn't even sure what continent Iraq was in. Then suddenly a picture popped into my head. I had no idea where it came from. It was of a mother tiger with her cubs. And a bunch of kids were nearby, looking scared. The cubs kept yelling, "You Fraidies!" at the kids.

What the heck did that have to do with rivers in Iraq?

Then I heard a voice inside my head. It said, *Tigress and you Fraidies*. That was it! The two biggest rivers in Iraq were the Tigris and the Euphrates! But how did I remember it? I quickly wrote down the answers.

I looked at the second question. "What is the tallest mountain in the world?" I was about to skip it. But then the answer popped inside my head again. Just like the last time. *Mount Everest.*

Wow! I was feeling great. I knew more than I thought I did!

I went on to the next question. "List the continents of the world in order of size." Oh, boy. I stopped feeling so smart. I knew Asia was pretty darn big. And I knew that North America and South America were continents. But was Australia a continent, or a really big island? And...

I didn't have to think any further. The voice in my head said, *Let's see...Asia, Africa, North America, South America, Antarctica, Europe, and Austral—*

At that exact moment I heard a snapping sound next to me. And the voice inside my mind said, *Darn pencil!* I turned around to see Spencer Sharp. He was holding a pencil with a broken point.

Spencer is the smartest kid in our class. He does math in his head that I can barely do on a calculator.

"Zack!" called out Mr. Snodgrass. "Eyes on our own papers, please!"

"Sorry," I said.

I sat back in my chair and gulped. The voice in my head belonged to Spencer! I hadn't remembered all those answers. I'd heard Spencer the way I'd heard Mrs. Krump. And now I knew what was going on. It all had started with that electric shock I got.

Holy guacamole! I could read people's minds!

This meant I'd been getting the test answers from Spencer Sharp. Not by looking at his paper, but by looking at his mind!

Question: Is reading somebody's mind cheating? I wasn't too sure about that. But just to be on the safe side, I decided not to listen anymore.

I tried humming. And I did my best to finish the rest of the test by myself. During a question on oceans I hummed a Beach Boys song. It was one my dad likes called "Catch a Wave." Still, I couldn't quite drown out the sound of Spencer's answers.

"Somebody appears to be humming," said Mr. Snodgrass. "Zack, is that you?"

"Uh, possibly," I said.

"Well, then, please be silent."

"Yes, sir," I said.

For a question about rain forests, I hummed a song we used to sing in day camp. "John Jacob Jingleheimer-Schmidt."

"Zack!" Mr. Snodgrass called out. "If you don't stop humming, you're going to have to give me your test paper now and leave the room."

"I'm sorry, sir," I said. "I won't do it anymore."

I tried to hum only in my head. But for the rest of the class, Spencer's thoughts kept bleeding through my humming.

"OK, time is up," said Mr. Snodgrass.

I was pretty sure I had gotten an A. But I felt funny about it. I saw that this mind reading stuff could be trouble.

Just how much trouble, I was about to find out.

Chapter 4

School was almost over. I went into my classroom to get my bookbag. Mrs. Coleman-Levin was at her desk with the pig's brain on it. She had no idea I could read minds! I looked around the room at the other guys in the class. None of them knew my powers!

As I turned my head, it was like tuning the knob on a radio. Little bits of what the kids were thinking came to me, separated by static:

...I can't believe how much homework I have...

...That pizza I had for lunch is still stuck in my stomach...

I couldn't tell who was thinking these things. But I knew it was all coming from kids in the room.

The door opened, and Floyd Hogmeister, the janitor, came in. The kids in my class are kind of scared of him. You know how they say some people have eyes in the back of their heads? Well, that's Mr. Hogmeister. He doesn't miss a thing—especially if a kid is doing something he shouldn't.

"I heard you had some trouble with an outlet," he said to Mrs. Coleman-Levin.

"Yes, Floyd," she said. "Zack must have shorted it out earlier in the day when he got an electric shock. I think you might need to replace it."

"I'll have a look-see," he said.

The janitor went to check the outlet that blew up when I got electrocuted. While he was doing that, I scanned the room. I was trying to pick up more bits and pieces of what people were thinking:

...Mom said not to eat too much candy after school. Is a pound too much?...

...I'm going to get an F on that geography test. And Dad's going to go crazy...

...Kill. Kill today? Kill now? No! Kill tomorrow!...

Whoa! What was this? Did I hear right? I jiggled my head. Then I scanned the room again.

...If I ask Spencer over, maybe he'll let me copy his homework...

...Is today the eighth day I've worn this underwear, or only the seventh? Tomorrow for sure I'll put on clean ones...

...I love to kill. Can't kill now. Wait till tomorrow. Kill tomorrow!...

There it was again! Who was thinking this? I finished stuffing my books into my bookbag. Then I looked around the room. I tried to act cool about it. But those thoughts sounded like somebody was plotting a murder. Could that be? Was one of the twenty kids in our class a crazy psycho killer?

No, I knew these guys. They might do stupid things, or even gross stuff. But kill somebody? No way.

Then my eyes came to rest on the janitor,

Mr. Hogmeister. Hmmmm. He sure was creepy. But a murderer?

I had no idea whose thoughts I was picking up. But I was worried. I thought I better check this out with my teacher.

I went up to Mrs. Coleman-Levin's desk. She was marking some papers, frowning.

"Could I speak to you a moment, Mrs. Coleman-Levin?" I asked.

She didn't look up from her pile of papers.

"I'm pretty busy now, Zack," she said.

"I'm sorry," I said. "It's kind of important."

She let out this really big sigh. Mrs. Coleman-Levin is not what you'd call a warm, fuzzy type.

"OK, shoot," she said.

I looked around. A lot of the kids were

staring at me. So was Mr. Hogmeister. His eyes fastened on to me like *he* was reading *my* mind. And I swear I heard him say, *This is the kid who shorted out the outlet. Little troublemaker. I'd better watch him.*

I smiled weakly at Mr. Hogmeister. Then I turned back to Mrs. Coleman-Levin.

"Perhaps I could speak to you outside?" I said.

"Outside? Why outside?"

"Because what I have to say is private," I said.

"OK," she said. "Follow me."

She clomped outside the classroom in her work boots. I followed her into the hall.

"What is it, Zack?"

"First, can I ask you a personal question, Mrs. Coleman-Levin?"

"Depends what it is," she said.

"Do you believe in ESP?"

"I don't know," she said. "I am a scientist. So I have an open mind. It's possible such things exist. Why do you ask?"

"Because I think today I learned how to read minds," I said.

"I see" was all she said.

"I've been listening to the thoughts of people in the classroom," I told her. "And I know this will sound unbelievable, but I think one of them is plotting a murder. Tomorrow!"

Mrs. Coleman-Levin looked at me very seriously.

"You're telling me you read the mind of a murderer?" she said.

I nodded. Then she took my hand and patted it. That is not like Mrs. Coleman-Levin at all.

From somewhere inside my head I

heard, *This kid is loony toons! Crazy as a bedbug.*

"I'm glad you told me this, Zack," she said. She was giving me this really sincere smile. "Tomorrow, let's keep our eyes and ears open. Maybe together we can discover who it is and stop him before he kills."

"Sure," I said.

Mrs. Coleman-Levin didn't believe a word I'd said.

"But for now," she said, "get yourself back in that classroom."

We went back in. A minute later the bell rang and Mrs. Coleman-Levin dismissed us.

"OK, everybody. Good-bye," she said. "I'm off to the morgue. But first, it's chow time for the snake. And on the menu today is a nice juicy mouse."

Mrs. Coleman-Levin had this really happy look on her face.

Boy, what a weirdo! I overheard one of the kids thinking as we filed out of homeroom. *She actually likes cutting up dead bodies.*

Hmmm. That got me thinking. Maybe Mrs. Coleman-Levin liked cutting up live bodies, too!

Chapter 5

When I got home, I decided to tell my dad what had happened. We've always been pretty close. But we've become even closer since my folks split up, and Dad got his own apartment. I can tell my dad anything at all. And he always understands.

"I don't understand," said my dad. "You say you think you can read people's minds?"

"No, Dad," I said. "I don't *think* I can. I *know* I can."

"I'm sorry, Zack," he said, "but that doesn't seem possible."

"Oh, it's possible, all right," I said.

"OK then. What am I thinking right now? Right this very minute?"

"Here is what you're thinking," I said. "Maybe the divorce is finally getting to me. Maybe you ought to send me to that child psychologist."

His mouth dropped open.

"How did you know that's what I was thinking?" he whispered.

"Dad, I already told you," I said. "I read minds. It happened in science class. I got an electric shock."

"OK, what am I thinking now?"

"You're hoping the psychologist is free

next Monday," I said. "Dad, trust me. This has nothing to do with the divorce."

He sighed and shook his head.

"This is amazing," he said. "Truly amazing. OK, what number am I thinking of?"

"Eighty-seven," I said. "Dad, I need your advice about something I heard in school. Somebody is plotting a murder."

He looked at me very seriously and narrowed his eyes.

"What animal am I thinking of?" he asked.

"A duck-billed platypus," I said impatiently. "Dad, didn't you hear what I said? *Somebody in school is plotting a murder.*"

"I'm sorry, Zack," he said. "It's just pretty incredible to find out your son is a

mind reader. But you nailed everything I was thinking. Including the eighty-seven and the duck-billed platypus. Now what's all this about somebody plotting a murder?"

"I picked up somebody's thoughts. They said they were going to kill someone. Tomorrow. I can't believe it could be one of the kids in my class. Maybe it's the janitor. He's very weird. Anytime we hang around his office in the basement, he yells at us. Once he said if we didn't stop bothering him, he'd kill us."

"Oh, that's just an expression," said my dad. "People say that kind of thing all the time. It doesn't mean they're killers."

Dad had a point. But if it wasn't Mr. Hogmeister, who was it? Mrs. Coleman-Levin?

"Dad, you've met Mrs. Coleman-Levin. Did she strike you as the murdering type?"

"Of course not. You're really being silly, Zack," Dad said with a wave of his hand. Then he focused his eyes on me. "OK, now. What famous singer am I thinking of? If you can do this every time, I could get you on *The Tonight Show*."

I tuned Dad out. It was clear he wasn't taking this seriously. But then, he hadn't heard that scary voice saying, "Kill...Kill!" Somebody's life was in danger. And I was going to have to solve this mystery on my own. So far I had two main suspects: Mr. Hogmeister and Mrs. Coleman-Levin.

And in case you're wondering which famous singer Dad was thinking of, it was Barry Manilow. Gross!

Chapter 6

I came to school wearing earmuffs the next day. I looked stupid in them. But I found it helped block out other people's thoughts.

Here's the thing about mind reading. Most of the stuff you learn, you wish you hadn't. Like Mrs. Taradash, the old lady who lives next door to us. I learned she would like to have a date with my dad. I found that out this morning in the elevator.

And Dad. I found out he hasn't been to the dentist in about two years. He makes me go every six months. It isn't fair!

I got to school half an hour early. That was so I could snoop around a little. It was scary having to track a killer by myself. But what else could I do? I couldn't go to the police. I mean what would I tell them? That I'd read the mind of somebody who was planning a murder? Somehow I didn't think they'd be too impressed with that.

I took off my earmuffs, went down to the basement, and hung around the janitor's office. Mr. Hogmeister was my number-one suspect. That was mainly because I didn't want it to be Mrs. Coleman-Levin. She may be weird, but I like her.

I could hear the sounds of heavy rain and thunder outside. A big storm was on its way. I'd heard that on the morning news. It made the basement seem even scarier. But I didn't let that stop me. I had to find out who the killer was before he killed.

I pretended to be picking up litter in the hallway. But I was hoping to pick up evil thoughts from Mr. Hogmeister. For several minutes, Mr. Hogmeister didn't have a single interesting thought. *My nose itches,* I heard. *I'll scratch it.* Then, *Mmmm, that feels good. Scratching is good. Especially if you itch. Not as good if you don't.* A second later I heard, *Outlet. Got to put in a new outlet. That kid Zack shorted out the old one. Dumb!*

So Mr. Hogmeister thought I was dumb, did he? Well, I didn't think he was exactly a genius. The question, though, was whether he was a killer.

I heard more thunder outside.

What was Mr. Hogmeister doing in there? I wished I could see. There was no keyhole in the door. But there was a little space between the door and the floor. I lay down and tried to peer under the door.

At first I didn't see anything at all. Then I saw a huge pair of feet. Then the feet started walking toward the door! Oh, no! I had to get up fast!

The door swung open. I scrambled to my feet. But I tripped and fell flat on my face. Mr. Hogmeister stood over me like a giant.

Thunder rumbled closer.

"What the heck are you doing?" he said in this really angry voice.

"Oh, hi there, Mr. Hogmeister," I said. I got up and slapped the dust off my shirt and pants.

"I said, what were you doing down there on the floor in front of my office?" he demanded.

"Uh, push-ups, sir," I said.

"What?"

"I was doing push-ups. I always do push-ups before class. To sort of wake myself up."

Mr. Hogmeister fastened his scary eyes on me. Then he leaned way down and pushed his face up close to mine. I think he must have eaten a garlic doughnut for breakfast! P.U.!

I was scared he was going to take a hammer and clonk me over the head. But instead he did something else. He started laughing. I had never seen Mr. Hogmeister laugh before. It was not a pretty sight.

Then I tuned in on his thoughts. *Push-*

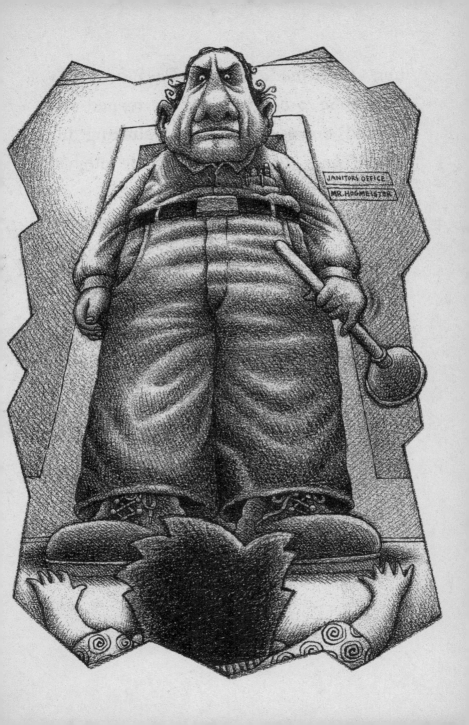

ups! *Give me a break! Does he really expect me to believe that?* He turned and walked down the hallway, shaking his head. *These kids—they kill me!* He laughed a weird laugh again.

I watched Mr. Hogmeister go. I was very puzzled. His thoughts didn't exactly sound like the thoughts of a murderer. Mr. Hogmeister was a weird guy, all right. But I was starting to think that maybe I should cross him off my list of suspects. Only, if I did that, then my number-one suspect was...Mrs. Coleman-Levin!

Chapter 7

Outside my classroom, rain was flinging itself against the windows. Lightning flashed. Thunder crashed. Mrs. Coleman-Levin was taking attendance. And then from somewhere I heard a strange voice. *Kill! Kill today!*

Mrs. Coleman-Levin was finished with attendance. Now she was standing up and walking over to my desk. She was looking right at me. I heard, *Kill this one when the time is right! How I crave the taste of blood!*

Yikes!

"Zack," said Mrs. Coleman-Levin, "could you eat lunch quickly today? Then I want you to come right back up here to the classroom." There was a strange expression on her face.

"Uh, wh-what for?" I stuttered.

"I need to talk to you."

"Alone, you mean?" I said, only it came out more like a squeak.

"Of *course* alone," she said. "I have a surprise for you."

I swallowed hard. I had a feeling I knew what the surprise was. Mrs. Coleman-Levin was a psycho killer, and I was her next victim. Some surprise! I had to get out of this. But how?

Between math and geography classes I

tried to phone Dad. I wanted him to come and take me home. But when I called him, his answering machine came on. Which is weird. My dad is always home. He's a writer, and that's where he works. But today, of all days, he was out. I left him a message. "Come and get me at school!" I said. "Right away!"

Then I went to Mrs. Krump's office. I told her I felt sick. If I stayed in her office, I'd be safe. But she took my temperature and said there was nothing wrong with me. She sent me back up to English class.

At lunch I sat at Spencer Sharp's table. And I heard him thinking he'd invite me to his birthday party next month at Actionland Amusement Park. That would have been nice. Too bad I might not be alive to enjoy it.

Mrs. Coleman-Levin had told me to eat

quickly. I was too scared to eat at all. The storm was really bad now. It was only 12:30. But it seemed as dark as night. And my dad hadn't shown up yet.

I was afraid to go upstairs to my classroom. But I had a plan. If Mrs. Coleman-Levin pulled anything funny, I would scream and run for my life. OK, so this wasn't a great plan. It was just the best one I could think of under pressure. But when I got up to the room, Mrs. Coleman-Levin wasn't even there.

It was creepy being all alone in the classroom. In the corner, the skeleton seemed to be grinning at me. Maybe once he'd been a student of Mrs. Coleman-Levin's, too.

I sat down at my desk to wait. There was a sudden clap of thunder. It was so loud I

actually jumped a couple of inches into the air. Right after that, all the lights went out.

Lightning must have knocked out the power. I was pretty freaked out, alone in the dark room.

Carefully I got up from my desk. From the flashes of lightning, I could almost see well enough to get to the door.

When I was about halfway there, I got this really creepy feeling. The feeling that I wasn't alone in the room. And right after that, I picked up a thought. It said, *There he is! Now I have him! The time to kill is now!*

Chapter 8

I screamed and rushed toward the door. Unfortunately, I tripped over a desk in the dark and came down hard on the floor. Pain shot through my knees.

Kill him! Kill him now! were the thoughts I heard in my ears.

Thunder exploded again outside. I started crying then. I have to admit it. I couldn't help it. You would have too, if you were me. If you don't think so, you're kidding yourself.

And just then the lights flickered on. I blinked in the glare. I looked around.

No one was there. Not a soul. So whose thoughts had I heard? I couldn't figure it out. Maybe I'd just imagined them. But just when I was beginning to think I was crazy, I heard them again. *He's trapped. Ready for the kill. Swallow him now!*

What? Wait a minute! *Swallow him?* What kind of killer could swallow a seventy-pound kid?

Out of the corner of my eye, I caught a quick motion. I turned and looked. Nothing. Just some fish in one of the tanks. And then I looked again.

No, not just some fish. The piranha. The

piranha was about to swallow a little fish! Mrs. Coleman-Levin must have put it in the piranha's tank at lunchtime. It was the piranha's thoughts I'd been receiving all along!

I sprang to the piranha tank. The piranha had trapped the little fish in the corner. With its jaws wide open, it was about to gulp him down.

I slapped the tank. Both fish jumped. I looked wildly around for a fishnet. Ah, there was one. I stuck it into the piranha tank and gently scooped up the little fish. Then I carried him to the fish tank and plopped him into it. The water splashed my hand.

From somewhere I heard the teeniest voice I've ever heard. It said, *A miracle! A miracle! Saved by the hand of God!*

On the floor near the piranha tank was a loose electric cord. It ran the filter motor in the aquarium. It must have yanked free when I slapped the tank to distract the piranha. I bent down and plugged it back in. I forgot my hand was wet.

There was a blue flash. My hand tingled all the way up my arm. Firecrackers went off in my eyes.

And then I blacked out.

Chapter 9

When I woke up, I was back on the cot in the nurse's office. Mrs. Krump and Mrs. Coleman-Levin were staring down at me. So was Dad.

"Oh, hi," I said.

"I found you on the floor of the classroom," said Mrs. Coleman-Levin. "How are you feeling?"

"Fine, thanks," I said. No, this time

I'd tell the truth. "Actually, not so hot," I said.

"You gave us quite a scare there, Zack," said my dad.

"I'm sorry," I said. "Pretty dumb of me to electrocute myself twice, huh?"

"I'm glad you're OK," said Mrs. Coleman-Levin.

I managed a smile. I was glad my homeroom teacher wasn't a psycho killer after all. I sat up.

"So what did you want to see me for?" I asked. "What was the surprise?"

"Oh, that," she said. "I decided to let a student take care of our tarantula over the vacation. I put everyone's name in a hat. And guess what? You won!"

"Uh...great...I guess," I said.

So that was the big surprise. Getting to

take care of a tarantula. Well, it was better than getting killed by a psycho murderer.

"Good," said Mrs. Coleman-Levin. "I thought that would make you happy. The important thing, though, is that you're safe." She patted my hand again.

I waited to hear what she really thought. I heard nothing. What was going on here?

And then it hit me. Getting shocked a second time must have knocked out my mind-reading powers. Was this possible? I had to check it out.

"Dad," I said, "think of a number between one and ten. Quick."

"OK, got it," he said. He turned to Mrs. Krump and Mrs. Coleman-Levin. "Watch this," he said. "Zack can read minds. It's amazing."

"You're not serious," said Mrs. Krump.

"I'm absolutely serious," said my dad. "Watch."

"The number you're thinking of is...five," I said.

"No," said my dad.

He looked at me and frowned in puzzlement.

"He usually gets it on the first guess," said my dad.

"The number you're thinking of is...ten."

"No," said my dad. He looked a little embarrassed.

"The number you're thinking of is...three?"

"No," said my dad.

"One?"

"No."

"Seven?"

"No. Zack, what's going on?"

"Six?"

"No."

"Eight?"

"No. Zack, what's happening here?"

"Dad, I think my powers are gone," I said.

"You should have seen him yesterday," said my dad.

Mrs. Krump and Mrs. Coleman-Levin just nodded. And even though I couldn't pick up their thoughts, I'm pretty sure they thought my dad and I were crazy.

So I'm not a mind reader anymore, and I don't really miss it. Not that much, anyway. Mind reading complicates your life too much. Now I'll just have to believe that people really mean what they say.

And, since I can't pick up answers from Spencer Sharp's mind anymore, I guess I'll have to really study for the English test next week.

What else happens to Zack?
Find out in
Through the Medicine Cabinet

Just as I was about to close the medicine cabinet door, something weird happened. Something very weird. The back of the medicine cabinet opened. And there, staring right in my face, was a boy who looked almost exactly like me!